MARY ENGELBREIT'S
LITTLE BOOK OF THANKS

HARPER
An Imprint of HarperCollinsPublishers

Library of Congress Control Number: 2020952882
ISBN 978-0-06-301721-4
Typography by Rachel Zegar
21 22 23 24 25 EP 10 9 8 7 6 5 4 3 2 1
❖
First Edition

I'm grateful for my friends, old and new,
whose love and care keep me going.

"As we express our gratitude, we must never forget that the highest appreciation is not to utter words, but to live by them."

—John F. Kennedy

"'Thank you' is
the best prayer that
anyone could say."

—Alice Walker

"I have a lot
to be thankful for.
I am healthy, happy
and I am loved."

—Reba McEntire

"What seem to us bitter trials are often blessings in disguise."

—Oscar Wilde

"Service to others is
the rent you pay
for your room
here on Earth."

—Muhammad Ali

" 'Tis the greatest wealth
to live content with little."

—Thomas Creech

"I feel extremely grateful
for this friendship."

—Alexandre Dumas

"Consider what is small
as great, and a few
as many."

—Lao-Tzu

"When I started counting
my blessings, my whole life
turned around."

—Willie Nelson

"I'm thankful for each
and every day."

—Chuck Berry

"Gratitude is the sign
of noble souls."

—Aesop

"Enjoy the little things,
for one day you may look
back and realize they
were the big things."

—Robert Brault

"Rest and be thankful."

—William Wordsworth

"This is a wonderful day.
I've never seen this one before."

—Maya Angelou

"I have perceiv'd
that to be with those
I like is enough."

—Walt Whitman

"When eating bamboo sprouts,
remember the one who planted them."

—Chinese Proverb

"Strive to give thanks."

—Rumi

"Everything has its
wonders, even darkness
and silence, and I learn,
whatever state I may
be in, to be content."

—Helen Keller

"I'm so thankful for friendship.
It beautifies life so much."

—L. M. Montgomery

"It is always so pleasant
to be generous."

—Ralph Waldo Emerson

"Let us be grateful
to the people who give
us happiness; they are the
charming gardeners who
make our souls blossom."

—Marcel Proust

"**D**on't let the sun
go down without saying
thank you to someone."

—Stephen King

"Happiness is the best thing
in the world."

—L. Frank Baum

"Let your last thinks
all be thanks."

—W. H. Auden